OOPS!

"Wow!" Randi cried. "Your dad ordered everything we saw on the computer, Anna! *Everything!*"

Anna looked puzzled. "Seems kind of strange . . . ," she muttered.

Woody scooped up an armful of leotards. "There's enough stuff here for ten pro shops!"

"Where are we going to put it all?" Randi asked.

"Beats me," Anna said. "The storeroom's almost full, and—" She clapped her hand over her mouth. Randi watched as her friend's face turned pale. "Uh-oh," Anna mumbled.

"What, Anna?" Randi and Woody asked together.

"Dad said he ordered skates, right? Just skates."

"Right," Randi agreed.

"So if Dad ordered just skates—"

"That means he didn't order all this," Woody finished.

"Maybe it's free. Like the trophies," Randi suggested.

"No way!" Anna cried. "Not all this stuff."

"Well, if it's not free," Randi said, "and if your dad didn't order it . . . who did?"

Don't miss any of the fun titles in the Silver Blades

FIGURE EIGHTS series!

ICE DREAMS

STAR FOR A DAY

THE BEST ICE SHOW EVER!

BOSSY ANNA

DOUBLE BIRTHDAY TROUBLE

SPECIAL DELIVERY MESS

and coming soon . . .

RANDI'S MISSING SKATES

Special Delivery Mess

Effin Older

Illustrated by Marcy Ramsey

Created by Parachute Press, Inc.

A SKYLARK BOOK

NEW YORK · TORONTO · LONDON · SYDNEY · AUCKLAND

RL 2.6, 006–009

SPECIAL DELIVERY MESS

A Skylark Book / January 1997

ISBN 0-553-48502-4

Published simultaneously in the United States and Canada

PRINTED IN THE UNITED STATES OF AMERICA

OPM   0 9 8 7 6 5 4 3 2 1

This book is for Ruth Older.

1

Click!

"Helping out in your dad's shop is so cool, Anna!" eight-year-old Randi Wong cried.

She reached down into a cardboard box and pulled out a handful of red, blue, and purple skate guards. She sorted and stacked them in neat piles on the counter.

"Yeah," Woody Bowen agreed. "We get to see all the new skating gear before anyone else!"

"Can I help you after school on Monday too?" Randi asked.

"You bet!" Randi's best friend, Anna Mullen, answered. "It's way more fun in Dad's shop with you two here."

Anna's parents were divorced, so Anna lived with her father, Toby Mullen. Mr. Mullen owned the pro shop at the Seneca Hills Ice Arena. Anna helped him in the shop on weekends and after school.

Randi loved hanging out with Anna and Woody, her best friends. The three of them practiced skating every Tuesday and Friday afternoon with their club, Figure Eights. On the days when there was no practice, Randi and Woody helped Anna in Mr. Mullen's pro shop.

Mr. Mullen sold everything a skater could want—warm-up outfits, skates, sweaters, sweatshirts, and fancy skating outfits. Randi loved the skating outfits best of all.

"Hey, I'll come back to help you too, Anna," Woody chimed in. He tucked his mop of red hair under his bright yellow baseball cap. "Monday I'll work the cash register."

Anna's long brown ponytail bounced as

she shook her head. "No way, Woody," she said. "Dad's the only one who touches the cash register."

"No fair!" Woody grumbled. "The cash register is the best part."

"Helping girls pick out skating outfits is the best part," Randi said. She tightened the purple scrunchies on her long black braids. "I'd love to have a new outfit for Figure Eights."

Randi pictured herself practicing her skating moves in a brand-new outfit.

"Dad's going to order more new outfits soon!" Anna reported. "We sold three of them this week!"

"Right!" Toby Mullen said, walking over to Anna. "Plus, we just sold three more. It's been the busiest Saturday in months!"

"Good thing we're all here to help you." Randi smiled at Mr. Mullen.

He grinned back. "You can say that again. I think I sold more skates today than ever before. Now that we're closed for the day, I'd better order some more." He moved toward his little office at the back of the shop.

"Dad, wait!" Anna called. "Can we watch you order?" She turned to Randi. "Wait until you see all the cool stuff Dad can order on the computer!"

"Sure, you can watch," Anna's father called back.

Randi couldn't wait to see this. She had played games on a computer. But she had never heard of using one to buy skates!

"First I'll go to the mall," Mr. Mullen said after he switched on the computer. "Then, when I'm in the mall, I'll go to the sporting goods store. That's where I'll buy the skates."

Randi looked confused. "You mean there's a whole mall in the computer?"

Mr. Mullen nodded. "Sort of. The computer lets you talk to all kinds of different stores. You can buy just about anything from them—baseballs, necklaces, toys. Whatever you want!"

Mr. Mullen put his hand on the computer mouse and clicked the button on it a few times. Randi watched as a picture of a huge shopping mall appeared on the screen. Mr. Mullen clicked some more. Each time he clicked, Randi saw a different shop on the screen.

"Hmmm. Hardware." *Click!* "Children's clothing." *Click!* "Ah, here it is—sporting goods!" Mr. Mullen announced. He ran his finger down a list of things for sale. "See, you can buy sweaters, skating outfits, leggings, skates, trophies—"

"Can we look at the outfits first, Dad?" Anna asked.

"Sure," Mr. Mullen said. He moved the mouse to a little box beside the word *Dresses*. He clicked.

On the screen, Randi saw a pink dress with a ruffled skirt. Mr. Mullen clicked again. A blue dress with white beads appeared. Then she saw a red dress covered with sparkling sequins.

"Wow!" Randi cried. "That red one is so beautiful!"

"Let's order it, Dad!" Anna said.

"Sorry, I'm not ordering dresses today, honey," Mr. Mullen told Anna. He clicked on a little box beside the word *Skates*. A pair of white figure skates appeared. "Now, let's see," he said. "I need ten pairs of size—"

"Excuse me, Toby," someone interrupted.

Randi glanced around. Mac, the handyman at the rink, stood in the doorway. He was dressed in blue denim overalls that were streaked with grease. "I'm having some trouble with the Zamboni again," he said. "And I need to clean the ice before the next session. Do you think you could give me a hand?"

"Sure thing, Mac. Be right there," Anna's father replied.

Randi thought it must be fun to ride on the huge Zamboni. It looked like a steamroller, and it made the ice on the rink nice and smooth.

Mr. Mullen clicked the mouse once more. Then he turned and left with Mac.

As soon as Mr. Mullen was out the door, Randi slid into his chair. "Hey! Let's look at that beautiful red dress again!"

Anna shook her head. "Uh-uh. We're not allowed to order on Dad's computer."

Randi rolled her eyes. "I don't mean *order* it. Just look at it."

"I don't think we should," Anna said.

"Why not?" Woody asked. "It's no big deal."

"Right," Randi agreed. "It won't hurt to look. I'll just click on the little boxes. Like your dad did."

Before Anna could say anything else, Randi pressed the button on the computer mouse. *Click!* The skates disappeared. Randi moved the mouse and clicked beside the word *Dresses.* A silver-and-blue dress with puffed sleeves blinked onto the screen.

"Wow!" Randi gasped. "Look at that! Let's see what else—"

"No, Randi!" Anna broke in. "We shouldn't be doing this!"

"Just a couple more," Randi pleaded. "It's so much fun!"

"Wait—it's my turn!" Woody cried, grabbing the computer mouse. *Click! Click! Click!*

Randi watched as skate guards, laces, pins, and trophies flashed by on the screen.

"Look! A Zamboni!" Woody yelled. "Mac would love this."

Randi looked up at the screen. Next to the picture of the Zamboni there were different buttons that let you choose how you wanted the Zamboni painted.

"Let's give the Zamboni blue-and-white stars!" Randi cried. Woody clicked the mouse button. The Zamboni on the screen now had blue-and-white stars all over it. "And how about some red-and-white stripes?" *Click!* Stripes appeared on the Zamboni.

"And since it's a present for Mac, let's have

it gift-wrapped!" Woody added. He moved the mouse to a box on the screen that said *Gift Wrap*. A big red bow now sat on top of the Zamboni. Randi and Woody giggled.

"Come on, you guys!" Anna cried. "My dad will be back any minute!"

"Just one more second," Randi begged. "Don't worry. It's not like we're doing anything wrong. We're just looking!"

"But you *are* doing something wrong!" Anna snapped. "I told you. We're not allowed to play on Dad's computer!"

"Let's just look at that red dress," Randi said. "Then we'll stop. Promise."

Randi clicked. The screen showed a white dress with a lacy skirt. "Whoa! That's the coolest! Check it out, Anna!"

Anna leaned over to study the outfit. "Yeah, it's—" She stopped short and looked up. "Yikes! I think I hear Dad coming!"

"No problem," Randi said calmly. "I'll just get us back to skates." She clicked, again and again. On the screen, leggings, sweaters, and trophies whizzed by. Everything but skates. Randi clicked furiously. "Uh-oh!" she cried. "Why can't I find them?"

"Hurry up, Randi!" Anna whispered. "Dad's coming!"

Randi clicked and clicked. "Skates . . . skates . . . where can they be?"

"Come *on*!" Anna urged. "He's almost here!"

"I can't find them. I just can't—" Randi stopped. "Yes!"

A pair of white skates appeared on the screen. Randi jumped out of the chair just as the bell over the pro shop door rang. A moment later Mr. Mullen walked into the office.

"See, Anna," Randi whispered. "There's nothing to worry about. Your dad will never know we touched his computer!"

2
Special Delivery!

"Hi, Mr. Mullen!" Randi called when she and Woody walked into the pro shop Monday afternoon. "Your helpers are back!"

"Hi, kids!" Anna's father answered. He was busy setting up a new display of leotards.

"Hey, Randi! Woody! Over here!" Anna yelled, poking her head out from behind a shelf. "I'm fixing this stack of T-shirts. You guys want to help?"

"Nah. Let's play on the computer," Woody whispered.

Anna rolled her eyes. "Very funny, Woody. If Dad ever found out what we did, he'd be furious!"

"Don't worry. He won't find out," Randi said. She grabbed a T-shirt and began to fold it carefully.

The bell over the pro shop door tinkled. "Special delivery!" Randi heard someone shout.

Randi turned around. A delivery man pushed a cart through the door. It was stacked high with boxes. "Big order for you, Mr. Mullen," the man said when he saw Anna's father.

"Must be the skates I ordered," Mr. Mullen called. "Anna, I'm busy with this display. Will you sign the delivery slip?"

Randi watched as Anna wrote her name in big, bold letters. It was *so* grown-up the way Anna signed the slip for her father.

"Come on, let's check out the new skates," Anna said after the delivery man had unloaded the boxes.

Randi and Woody helped Anna pull the boxes into the storeroom. They opened box after box. Each one had dozens of brand-new skates. Finally they got to the last box.

"Whew! I'm glad this is the last one," Randi said, opening the lid. "I'm tired!"

But this box wasn't filled with skates.

"Hey! Look at *this*!" Randi cried. She held up a shiny silver trophy. On the top there was a skater standing on one foot. She held her other foot high over her head.

"I didn't know Dad ordered trophies," Anna said. She called to her father. "Hey, Dad! Did you order trophies?"

"Nope. Just skates," her father called back. "Whoops! Four o'clock! I promised Mac I'd help him get the Zamboni started before the evening session. Can you kids handle things here for a few minutes?"

"Uh . . . no problem," Anna answered. Randi heard the bell over the pro shop door ring as Mr. Mullen left.

"So, where did these come from?" Randi

asked. She reached into the box and pulled out two more shiny silver trophies.

Anna looked thoughtful. "You know what? I bet they came as a bonus for ordering all those skates. Sometimes the skate company sends Dad free things when he sends in a big order."

Woody nodded. "Yeah. Once my mom bought new cooking pots. They gave her two packages of spaghetti with the pots. Free."

"So, if they're free, your dad won't care if we each take one, will he?" Randi asked.

Anna shrugged. "Guess not."

"Cool!" Woody yelled. He chose a trophy with a skater doing a flying camel spin.

Anna picked one with two skaters dancing. "Let's stack the rest of the trophies and skates on the shelves," she suggested.

They had just finished stacking the last three trophies when Randi heard a voice call out, "Special delivery!"

This time four delivery men walked

through the pro shop's door. And each one held three boxes!

"Stack them here, please. By the counter," Anna told the men. "The storeroom's almost full."

"This is like having a giant birthday party!" Randi cried when the delivery men were gone. She ripped open the cover of one of the boxes. Her jaw dropped. "Look, Anna! It's the same dress we saw on the computer! The red one with the sequins!"

Anna dug deeper into the box. She held up a silver-and-blue dress with puffed sleeves. "We saw this one, too!" she exclaimed.

Woody opened another box. "And these!" He held up a bunch of skate guards.

"What else is in these boxes?" Anna asked.

Randi, Woody, and Anna tore through the cartons. When they were finished, there were dresses, skirts, sweaters, leotards, laces, pins, and badges all over the pro shop.

"Wow!" Randi cried. "Your dad ordered

everything we saw on the computer, Anna! *Everything!*"

Anna looked puzzled. "Seems kind of strange . . . ," she muttered.

Woody scooped up an armful of leotards. "There's enough stuff here for ten pro shops!"

"Where are we going to put it all?" Randi asked.

"Beats me," Anna said. "The storeroom's almost full, and—" She clapped her hand over her mouth. Randi watched as her friend's face turned pale. "Uh-oh," Anna mumbled.

"What, Anna?" Randi and Woody asked together.

"Dad said he ordered skates, right? Just skates."

"Right," Randi agreed.

"So if Dad ordered just skates—"

"—that means he didn't order all this," Woody finished.

"Maybe it's free. Like the trophies," Randi suggested.

"No way!" Anna cried. "Not all this stuff."

"Well, if it's not free," Randi said, "and if your dad didn't order it . . . who did?"

3
Squiggly Fish

"**Y**ou did, Randi! I told you to stay off Dad's computer, but *you wouldn't listen!*" Anna declared.

Randi gulped. "Me? *I* ordered all this stuff?"

"Yes," Anna said. "When you and Woody were fooling around on Dad's computer."

Randi scrunched up her nose. "But . . . but I wasn't *ordering*. I was just looking."

"You *thought* you were just looking, but every time you and Woody clicked, you must have ordered something," Anna explained.

Woody pointed his finger at Randi. "*She*

19

clicked more than I did. *Randi* ordered most of the stuff."

Randi narrowed her eyes. "Don't try to get out of this, Woody. It's your fault too!"

But it's mostly *my fault,* Randi admitted to herself. *It was* my *idea to look at the skating outfits again. It was* me *who didn't listen when Anna told us to get off the computer.*

"I'm going to be in big trouble," Anna said. "When Dad sees all this, I'm doomed!"

"Then he *won't* see it!" Randi cried. "We'll send it back! We'll send it all back to wherever it came from." She started digging furiously through the piles of boxes. "There's got to be an address here somewhere. Help me find it!"

Woody and Anna helped Randi check every box, inside and out. But they couldn't find an address anywhere.

"Hey! Maybe the address is on the computer!" Woody cried.

"*Don't* touch the computer again!" Anna warned.

"We've got to, Anna," Randi insisted.

She scrambled over the huge piles of clothes into the back office. She sat down at the computer. Brightly colored fish squiggled back and forth across the black screen. "What's with the fish, Anna?" Randi asked.

"That means the computer's on," Anna said. "Press a button. I think they'll go away."

Randi held her finger above the keyboard. "I hope I'm not ordering fish," she muttered. *Click!* The fish disappeared. Words came onto the screen. Weird words like *Font* and *Format*. Randi clicked again. Back came the squiggly fish. Where was the shopping mall?

Randi slumped in her chair. "Dumb computer. All it has is fish!" She looked at Anna and Woody. "What are we going to do?"

"We're telling Dad, that's what," Anna said.

Randi's heart sank. Every time she came to the pro shop, she tried so hard to show Mr. Mullen what a good helper she could be. *If he finds out what I did he'll never let me in his shop again,* she thought.

"No, Anna! Please don't tell your father!" she begged. "I know I can think of another way out of this."

"Like what?" Anna asked.

Randi sat still for a minute. She thought hard. Nothing came to mind. "I'm not sure yet, but you have to give me a chance. Let's hide everything until I can think of something!"

Anna looked doubtful. "*Where* would we hide it all? The storeroom is already crammed full of skates and trophies."

Randi thought again. "Well . . . there's Harry's Snack Bar next door. And the locker room. And—"

"And my mom's office," Woody added.

Mrs. Bowen worked in an office across from the pro shop. She was president of Silver Blades, the skating club that Randi's older sister Jill belonged to. The office had a huge closet.

"We'll use all those places!" Randi cried. "Woody—you take some of the stuff to your mother's office. Anna—you and I will take some to the girls' locker room and to Harry's." Randi high-fived her two friends. "Let's go!"

At top speed, they piled everything back into the boxes.

Dragging the heavy boxes behind them, Randi, Anna, and Woody wobbled out the pro shop door.

When they reached the locker room, Randi shoved open the door, and Anna pushed the boxes in. Then the two of them went to work, stuffing everything into an empty locker.

"There," Randi said, closing the door. "It's all hidden."

"But Randi, what about all *that* stuff?"

Randi turned around. Anna pointed to one more big box over by the door. It was still full of skating gear. "Oh, no!" Randi cried. "The locker is full!"

"We've got to cram these in, too," Anna said.

"Okay," Randi said. "You stuff while I close the door."

Anna shoved the clothes into the locker. Randi pushed against the door with all her weight. "It won't close!" she wailed.

"We'll push together," Anna said. "One, two, three, push!"

Grunting and groaning, Randi and Anna pushed against the door. Finally it snapped shut. "Whew!" Randi whispered. "That wasn't easy. Now let's get those other boxes over to Harry's like we planned."

Randi and Anna hurried back to the pro shop. They each grabbed a box and dragged it across the hall to Harry's Snack Bar.

"Presents? For me?" Harry joked when he saw Randi and Anna.

"Uh, not exactly," Randi said. She nearly tripped over the big box at her feet. "They're a . . . a . . . surprise."

24

"Yes. A surprise for my dad," Anna added quickly.

"And we were wondering if we could . . . if we could hide them in here." Randi swallowed hard.

Harry tugged on his bushy white beard. "Hmmm. I think I can help you out."

Harry lifted the boxes off the floor. Randi watched him stack them behind the sandwich counter. "Thanks, Harry," she said. She touched her finger to her lips. "Remember, it's a surprise. Don't tell!"

Harry winked. "Gotcha!"

Randi and Anna raced back to the pro shop. Woody was waiting for them.

"How did it go, Woody?" Randi asked.

"Cool!" Woody answered. "I told Mom it was her birthday present. A really *big* birthday present. She promised not to look."

Randi wrinkled her nose. "Your mom just had a birthday."

Woody chuckled. "I said it was for next year!"

"Well, at least we've hidden everything," Randi said. She gave a long sigh of relief.

"Uh . . . no, we haven't," Woody said. He piled a bunch of skating outfits into Randi's arms.

"Oh, no!" she cried. "How did we forget these?"

"Shhh!" Anna whispered. She tiptocd to the door. "Here comes Dad!"

"But what about these outfits?" Randi whispered back.

Anna dashed behind the counter. She pulled out a big green shopping bag. "Quick! Put them in herc!"

Randi shoved the outfits into the bag. She crammed the last one in just as the bell over the pro shop door tinkled.

Mr. Mullen walked into the shop. "No problems while I was gone?" he asked.

Randi stood as still as a statue. She tried to hide the big green bag behind her legs.

"Uh, n-no problems, D-Dad," Anna stammered. "Everything's fine."

Mr. Mullen smiled. "Good. I'll go check out the new skates in the storeroom." He hurried to the back of the store.

"Whoa!" Anna said. "That was *too* close!" She snatched the green shopping bag and shoved it into Randi's arms. "Dad might find this if we leave it here. You've got to take it home."

"But—But what if someone asks me—" Randi protested.

"Take it!" Anna insisted.

The pro shop door opened again. Randi's sister Jill walked in. "Hey, Randi. My lesson just finished," Jill said. "I have to get some stuff from my locker. Meet me in the lobby in five minutes and we'll head home, okay?"

"Okay," Randi answered. She gathered all her things, along with the huge bag of outfits.

"See you guys tomorrow," she called to her friends as she left.

Randi found Jill waiting in the lobby. "I'm ready, Jill!" she said brightly. "Let's go!"

"Wait a minute!" Jill said. "What's in the bag?"

4

Gotcha!

"Uh . . . nothing," Randi answered nervously. She tried to sound calm, even though her heart was pounding. "I mean, just some skating outfits Anna asked me to hold for her."

Anna did *tell me to take the dresses,* Randi thought. *So it's not like I'm lying.*

"Anna's probably got a whole closet full of outfits from her father's shop," Jill said. She sighed. "I wish I could have a new dress for my competition next week. . . ."

Randi asked Jill all about her program for the competition. She loved hearing about the spins and jumps Jill was working on.

When they reached the house, Jill walked straight into the kitchen. Randi could hear their mother inside, singing an ABC song to their three-year-old sister, Laurie.

From the dining room Randi heard *"Va-room, va-room! Va-room, va-room!"* She peeked in and saw her six-year-old twin brothers, Michael and Mark, playing with their toy trucks.

Randi crept down the hallway. *Yippee! The coast is clear! No one will see me with the shopping bag and start asking questions.*

She tiptoed up the carpeted stairs. The bag bumped softly against her legs. She was almost to the top stair when something grabbed her ankle!

"Yeeooww!" she yelled.

"Gotcha!"

Randi didn't have to turn around. She knew who it was. Her twelve-year-old, pain-in-the-neck brother, Henry!

"Where are you going?" Henry asked.

"To my room," Randi said. "Now let go of my ankle."

"What's in the bag?" Henry continued, ignoring her.

"None of your business," Randi answered.

With his free hand, Henry grabbed the bag. "What's in it? Let me see or I'll tell Mom you won't show me."

"No way, Buffalo Brain!" Randi yelled. She held on tightly to the bag. "Now, let go!" She felt her face get hot. *Why couldn't Henry live in another city? Or better yet, on another planet!*

"*You* let go!" Henry snorted. He yanked the bag.

Randi yanked too.

The bag slipped out of Randi's hand. She watched in horror as all the beautiful outfits spilled out onto the stairs.

Henry grabbed one of them. "Hey! Where did you get these? You couldn't have bought

them all!" His eyes opened wide. "Randi, did you *steal* these?"

"What!" she cried. "I don't steal!"

"Then where did you get them?" he asked.

"From Anna. They're a . . . a surprise for Mr. Mullen. A special delivery surprise." She looked her brother straight in the eye. "And since it's a surprise, you have to promise not to tell anyone. Promise?"

Henry smiled. "Maybe. Maybe not."

"*Promise,* Henry!" Randi demanded. "Promise, or . . . or I'll tell everybody in your class that you love Gina Glover." Now Randi started to smile.

"What? I *hate* Gina Glover!" Henry snarled. "She's so stuck-up!"

"*I* know that," Randi said sweetly. "But I'll *still* tell everybody in your class that you love her . . . unless you promise."

Henry frowned. "I promise," he muttered. He turned and ran down the stairs.

Randi dashed into the bedroom she shared

with Laurie. She closed the door tight so that no one would sneak up on her again.

Randi slid the silver trophy out of her backpack. She placed it carefully on her dresser. Then she looked around the room, trying to decide where to hide the dresses. Should she hide them in her closet? In her dresser? Under her bed?

No! Randi thought. *I'll hide them in Laurie's toy closet!* She opened the door. Books, games, dolls, and stuffed animals tumbled out. Randi smiled. *Perfect. A big fat mess! No one will notice a bag of outfits in all this junk.*

She shoved the green shopping bag into the back corner of Laurie's closet. Then she piled everything on top. "Now I'd better get downstairs and help Mom with dinner," she said aloud.

She bounded down the stairs and into the kitchen. Jill and their mom were still there.

"But I really need a new dress for the competition," Randi heard Jill say. "My old one doesn't fit right. And this one is *perfect*." Jill held up a piece of paper. Randi could just make out the photo of a skater on it.

"I'm sure your old outfit looks just fine," Mrs. Wong said as she rolled hamburger into little round meatballs.

"Hi, Mom!" Randi said.

"Hi, honey!" Mrs. Wong answered.

"Please, Mom," Jill continued. "Kathy says the way you look when you compete is really important."

Randi knew Kathy Bart. She was Jill's skating coach in Silver Blades.

"Kathy says that having confidence is as important as being able to do perfect jumps and spins," Jill went on. "How can I have confidence competing in a dress that's getting too small for me?"

Mrs. Wong stopped rolling meatballs. She turned to Jill. "You know we'd like you to have a new dress, but we just don't have the money right now. You understand, don't you?"

Jill hung her head. "I guess so," she mumbled. She dropped the piece of paper on the table and walked out of the kitchen. Randi felt sad for Jill. She wanted to help her sister.

But what can I do? she asked herself. *I don't have enough money to buy Jill a new dress.*

Randi trudged over to the kitchen table. She picked up the paper Jill had dropped— and gasped. *Maybe there is something I can do!*

Randi ran upstairs with the paper held tightly in her hand. She threw open Laurie's toy closet and pulled out the big green shopping bag. "Where is it?" she muttered as she dumped the outfits onto her bed.

Then she stopped. The beautiful red skating outfit glittered on the top of the pile. Randi looked down at the picture in her hand, then back at the outfit on her bed. She couldn't believe it! She had the *exact* outfit that Jill wanted!

If I can find a way to keep it, I can give Jill

this *dress,* Randi thought. *It will make Jill feel confident, and then she'll skate like a champion!*

All I have to do is find some way out of this special delivery mess!

5

No-Mistakes Max

The next morning at Grandview Elementary, Randi sat with Anna and Woody on the swings. They were waiting for the first bell to ring.

Randi pushed herself back and forth. "Come on, you guys. We've got to think of some way out of this special delivery mess."

"Hey! Here come Max and Kate!" Woody yelled. "Let's ask them to help. We can trust them. And maybe Max can come up with a scientific solution!"

Max Harper and Kate Alvaro both skated in Figure Eights.

Max was also the biggest brain in the fourth grade. He was great at science. He was even better at computers.

"Well . . . okay," Randi agreed. "But they have to promise they won't tell."

"Hey, guys!" Woody yelled. "Come here! We need your help!" Woody told Max and Kate the whole story. Then he made them promise to keep it a secret.

Max pushed his blond bangs off his glasses. "I promise I won't tell anyone about the delivery," he said.

"Me too," Kate said. "But what's the problem? Why don't you just send all the stuff back?"

Woody sighed. "We tried to. We couldn't figure out how."

"How about putting up a For Sale sign? On the bulletin board at the rink?" Kate suggested.

"No way!" Anna exclaimed. "Dad might see it."

"Well, if you can't send the order back, and you can't put up a For Sale sign, then my only other idea is—"

"What, Kate?" Randi asked.

"Is to tell Mr. Mullen. Just tell him," Kate said.

"*That's* your idea?" Randi moaned. "Forget it! You don't understand how angry Mr. Mullen would be if he knew what we did." She hid her face in her hands.

"Sor-ry," Kate mumbled. "*I* thought it was a good idea." She sat down on the grass with her back to Randi.

Max snapped his fingers. "I know! I'll send a message on the computer!"

Randi peeked out between her fingers. "What do you mean?"

"I talk to kids on the computer all the time," Max said. "I send them messages and they write back. I'll tell them about the stuff and see if they want to buy it. Cool idea, huh?"

Randi looked doubtful. "I . . . I don't know. What if we make another computer mistake and—"

Max poked himself in the chest. "Hey! All the kids I talk to ask *me* computer questions. They call me No-Mistakes Max."

"Well . . . all right, Max," Randi finally said. "When can we send the message?"

"We can't use my computer. My dad is putting a new chip into it for me. But how about we meet in the pro shop this afternoon, after Figure Eights practice? We'll go to the computer, and—"

"Forget it!" Anna shook her head. "No one touches Dad's computer anymore!"

"But Anna—" Randi began.

"No! And that's final," Anna said, crossing her arms. "Look what happened the last time!"

Randi hated to admit it, but Anna was right. Even if they did have No-Mistakes Max helping them, something might go wrong on Mr. Mullen's computer.

"My mom has a computer in her office," Woody said. "We could use that one . . . if we can think of a way to get her out of there."

Everyone thought hard. "I'm stumped," Woody said.

"Me too," Kate added glumly.

"Hey, I've got an idea!" Randi burst out. She lowered her voice. "But I'll need some help. Especially from Woody!"

Randi whispered her idea to everyone.

Woody leaped off the swing. "Forget it! I'm not doing it!"

"You have to, Woody!" Randi snapped. "Don't forget, *you* ordered some of the stuff. *You're* in trouble, too."

"But your idea is so dumb!" Woody whined.

"*You* didn't come up with anything smarter!" Randi shot back.

Brriinng! The first bell sounded.

Woody sighed heavily. "Okay. I'll do it— but I won't like it!"

6

Bunny Flop!

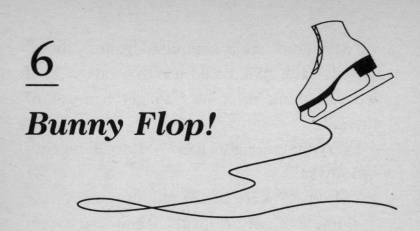

"Over here!" Randi's coach called to everyone in Figure Eights that afternoon. She waved from the far end of the rink.

Randi glided across the ice. All her friends gathered around Carol Crandall. Anna, Kate, and Josh Freeman stood on one side of her. Woody, Max, Samantha Rivers, and Frederika Hamilton waited on the other.

Randi slid to a stop between Anna and Kate.

"Guess what!" Carol said, smiling. "Today you'll be learning your first jump."

"Yay! Cool! Awesome!" everyone in Figure Eights shouted. Randi shouted loudest of all. She couldn't wait to learn jumps.

"Your first jump is called the bunny hop," Carol said.

"You mean we hop up and down *while we're skating*?" Kate asked. "No way! I'll never be able to do that!"

Samantha shook her dark, frizzy hair. "Me either."

Woody chuckled. "You two can do the bunny *flop*!"

Everybody groaned at Woody's dumb joke.

"*I'm* not doing it!" Frederika snapped. "I might fall and get ice all over my new outfit."

Everybody groaned again.

"She has a zillion new outfits," Randi whispered to Anna. "So what if she messes one up?"

"You'll all love the bunny hop," Carol said. "Watch. I'll show you how to do it."

Randi watched as Carol pushed off on her left foot. Then she kicked her right foot out front and—*hop!* She landed on her right toe pick and glided on her left foot again.

"The most important thing is to land on your right toe pick and flat on your left blade," Carol said.

"Cool! Want to practice with me?" Randi asked Anna.

Anna was the best skater in Figure Eights. Randi loved practicing with her.

"Sure," said Anna. "Let's go!"

Randi and Anna pushed off, side by side. They glided left. They kicked their right skates out to the front. They hopped. Anna landed on her right toe pick.

"Ow!" Randi yelped. *She* landed on the cold, hard ice!

"Good try, Randi!" Carol called. "Don't forget—land on your right toe pick."

"Okay," Randi answered. "I'll remember next time." She stood up and brushed ice chips off her yellow leggings.

Randi practiced the bunny hop over and over. She was having so much fun, she forgot all about her plan to fix the special delivery mess. Until she looked at her watch. Only five minutes left in the lesson! Why didn't Woody start the plan?

Just then Anna and Max skated over to Randi. "Lesson's almost done," Max whispered. "What is Woody waiting for?"

Randi put her hands on her hips. "I don't know. If he backs out now, he's going to ruin everything!"

Then Randi heard a yell. She turned around. Across the rink, Woody landed flat on the ice. He moaned and held his knee.

"Sounds like he's really hurt!" Anna cried.

Randi, Max, and Anna raced over to Woody. So did Carol and the rest of the Figure Eights.

Woody's moans filled the rink. They echoed off the walls. "Ohhh," he moaned. "Ohhh, ohhh, ohhh." His eyes were squeezed tight.

"What happened, Woody?" Carol asked, hurrying over to him.

He pointed to his knee. "Hurt. Hurt bad. Bunny hop."

Carol bent over Woody. "You hurt your knee? But I saw you fall. I thought you landed on your bottom."

"Noooo. Knceee," Woody wailed. "Get . . . my . . . mommm."

Randi stared at Woody's face. He gave Randi a smile. It was a teeny-tiny smile. But Randi saw it. So did Anna, Kate, and Max. Randi bit her lip to keep from laughing.

Yes! Randi thought. *Woody did it! Now for the rest of the plan!*

Woody squeezed his eyes shut again. "Mommm," he moaned.

"Someone go get Mrs. Bowen," Carol called over her shoulder.

"I will!" Max yelled. He took off for Mrs. Bowen's office.

Go, Max! Randi cheered silently. *Get Woody's mom out of her office and send that message!*

Woody moaned more and more loudly.

Mrs. Bowen appeared at the edge of the ice in seconds.

"Here comes your mom, Woody," Randi said. She looked up at Carol. "Our lesson is over, right?"

Carol nodded. Her brow was creased with worry. "Uh . . . sure. See you Friday."

Randi stood up. She sped across the ice after Kate and Anna. They were all trying so hard to keep from laughing that they could barely pull on their skate guards.

"I hope Woody keeps moaning long enough for Max to send the message," Randi said.

Randi, Kate, and Anna raced over to Mrs. Bowen's office.

"Here it is," Max declared the moment they stepped into Mrs. Bowen's office.

"You mean it's all done?" Randi asked.

"Yup," Max said. "Read it for yourself."

Randi stepped over to the screen and read Max's message: TOTALLY COOL ICE-SKATING GEAR FOR SALE. SKATES, SKATE GUARDS,

T-SHIRTS, ETC. INTERESTED? SEND A MESSAGE TO MAX.

Max took hold of the mouse. He moved it to the box on the screen that read *Send*. He clicked, and the message disappeared.

"Now we wait and see if anyone answers," Max said.

Randi stared at the computer screen. She clasped her hands together. "Please answer," she begged out loud. "Please, please, please!"

7

Woody's Act

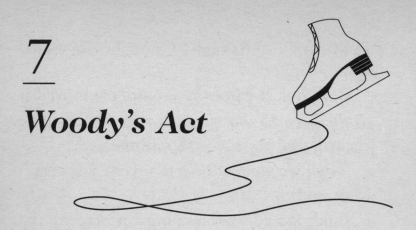

"**Y**ou were so funny, Woody!" Randi laughed so hard she had to hold on to Kate to keep from falling over. "I want my mommm! I want my mommm!" she mimicked, wiping away fake tears.

It was Friday afternoon. Randi stood outside Mrs. Bowen's office with Woody, Kate, Anna, and Max. Their Figure Eights lesson would start in half an hour.

Max put his hand on Woody's shoulder. "That was some act," he said. "You had *me* fooled."

"Me too," Anna said. "I thought you really hurt yourself."

Woody chuckled. "Yeah, I guess I'd make a pretty good actor." He pulled his yellow baseball cap low on his head. "Now, excuse me. It's time for my next act."

"Right," Randi said. "You've got to get your mother away from her computer again, so Max can check to see if anyone answered our message."

"No problem," Woody said. "I've got it all figured out. Watch this." He strolled into his mother's office.

"We'll wait out here," Anna called from the hall.

"What are you doing in here, Woody?" Randi heard Mrs. Bowen ask. "Don't you have your Figure Eights lesson?"

"Yup. In half an hour. But I've been thinking—"

"About what?"

"About *you*, Mom," Woody said. "I've

been thinking that . . . well, you're the best mom in the whole world. And because you're *so* great, I want to take you to Harry's. For one of his special double-chocolate shakes."

"I see," Mrs. Bowen said.

Randi thought Woody's mom sounded a little suspicious. She peeked through the door. Mrs. Bowen *looked* a *lot* suspicious.

"How about it, Mom?" Woody asked.

"Well . . . I'm pretty busy, and—"

"Too busy for *me*?"

Randi giggled. Woody sounded so hurt.

Mrs. Bowen didn't say anything for a long time. Randi held her breath. *Can Woody do it?* Randi worried. *Can he get his mom to leave her office?*

Mrs. Bowen finally answered, "You're up to something, Woody. But I love Harry's chocolate shakes. Sure, let's go!"

"Yes! He did it!" Randi whispered to her friends. They waited until Woody and his mother had left. Then they dashed inside.

Max sat down at the computer and began clicking away.

"So, how many messages did we get?" Randi asked impatiently. She hoped there would be hundreds.

Max clicked some more. He gazed thoughtfully at the screen, but he didn't say anything.

"Come on, Max! How many?" Randi asked again.

Max turned around. "No messages," he said. "None at all."

"None at all!" Randi repeated. "Are you sure?"

"None," Max declared.

"Okay—that's it!" Anna cried. "We tried hiding the stuff. We tried getting rid of it. Nothing worked. Now I'm telling Dad!"

"No, Anna!" Randi begged. "Not yet! I'll think of something. I know I will!"

Anna looked doubtful. "Today is Friday," she said. "The bill for the special delivery will probably come on Monday. If you can't think of something by then, we *have* to bring all the stuff back to the pro shop. And we have to tell Dad."

"But Anna—" Randi heard a whistle. "That's Woody's signal!" she yelled. "They're coming back!"

"Yikes! Mrs. Bowen is going to catch us here!" Kate wailed.

"I have to stop Woody! He has to stall his mom!" Randi cried. She poked her head out the door, just enough for Woody to see her . . . if he was looking in her direction.

He was!

Woody stared at Randi for a second. His eyes went wide. Then he grabbed his mother's arm and whirled her around.

"Wha—What are you doing, Woody?" Randi heard Mrs. Bowen ask.

"We've got to go back to Harry's," Woody told her. "I . . . forgot my baseball cap. You have to help me find it."

Mrs. Bowen began walking back to

Harry's. "This can't take too long, Woody. I have to get back to work," she said.

"Come on!" Randi whispered. "Let's get out of here!"

"We didn't get *one* message?" Woody asked when he stepped onto the ice a few minutes later. "Major bummer!"

Carol glided out onto the ice. "Bunny hoppers!" she called. "Ready to practice?"

"Ready!" everyone in Figure Eights answered. Everyone except Randi. Her plan had failed. What was she going to do now?

"Let's play Follow the Leader," Carol said. "It's a great way to practice our bunny hops. Everybody line up behind me. When I hop, you hop. Ready?"

Randi lined up. But she didn't feel like hopping. Anna had given her until Monday to think of something. But Monday was just two days away. Two short days. What was she going to do?

8

Say Cheese!

After the Figure Eights bunny hop lesson, Randi and Jill walked home from the rink.

"Are you excited about your competition next week, Jill?" Randi asked her sister.

"I'd be more excited if I had a new outfit," Jill answered.

Randi wished she could tell Jill about the red outfit. And about how she was trying to make sure Jill could have it.

But Anna had told her to bring *all* the dresses back on Monday—including Jill's—unless Randi could think of a way to keep the red one. And so far, she hadn't thought of one thing.

When Randi got home, she went straight upstairs to her bedroom. She pulled the big green shopping bag out of Laurie's closet. A blue-and-silver dress with puffed sleeves lay on top. Right next to Jill's red one.

It's so beautiful, Randi thought, lifting the blue-and-silver outfit from the bag. *I wish I could have it. But I know I can't.* She started to put the dress back. Then she stopped. Her heart began to pound. *I guess it wouldn't hurt to try it on.*

Quickly Randi slipped out of her purple sweatshirt and leggings. She wriggled into the blue-and-silver dress. She stared at herself in the mirror. *Wow! I look like a champion!*

Randi stretched her arms above her head. She pointed her toe and smiled at herself. Then she got into position for the bunny hop. She was in the middle of her hop when the door burst open.

Randi jumped. Her ten-year-old sister, Kristi, walked into the room.

"Sorry, Randi. I didn't mean to scare you," Kristi said. "Hey! Where did you get that dress?"

"From . . . From Anna," Randi stammered. "But I'm not keeping it. I'm just trying it on."

"You look cool. Want me to take your picture?" Kristi asked.

"Would you?" Randi said. "My camera is here somewhere." She pushed aside books, puzzles, games, and stuffed animals on her shelf. Underneath she found her little camera. "Here it is."

Kristi took the camera and put it up to her eye.

"Wait!" Randi yelled. She picked up the trophy on her dresser. "I'll pretend I won this!"

Kristi started to take the picture again. She stopped. "Hey!" she cried. "There's too much junk behind you. Stand in front of one of your posters instead."

Randi's wall had posters of skating champions all over it. Randi scooted in front of the one of Nicole Bobek.

"That's better," Kristi said. She snapped the picture.

"Oh, I can't wait to see what I look like!" Randi said.

"You look like twins."

Randi frowned. "Who looks like twins?"

Kristi pointed to the poster. "You and Nicole. You're both wearing the same kind of outfit!"

Randi looked behind her. Kristi was right! Her outfit looked almost exactly like Nicole Bobek's!

"Oops, I almost forgot," Kristi said. "I came to get you. It's your turn to set the table for dinner." She set the camera on Randi's dresser and started out the door.

"Be right down," Randi called. "Hey,

Kristi! Don't tell anybody about the dress, okay?"

"My lips are sealed," Kristi answered.

Randi smiled as she studied the poster. "I *do* look like a champion! I can't wait to show my picture to Anna. I bet she'd like a picture like that." Randi stopped. "That's it!" she cried. "That's what I'll do!"

Randi ran downstairs to the phone. She punched in Anna's number. "Meet me on Sunday at the rink," she said when Anna answered. "I'm going to ask Kate, Max, and Woody to come too."

"But it's too crowded to skate on Sunday," Anna reminded Randi.

"It's not for skating," Randi answered mysteriously. "It's for something else! Something really important!"

"Okay," Anna agreed. "I'll be there."

Randi hung up the phone. *If my idea works, I'll be able to pay for the special delivery—and Jill's new dress!* she thought. If *it* works!

9

Randi's Plan

"There," Randi said as she taped the last poster to the wall of the girls' locker room. "That makes six posters."

It was Sunday afternoon. Randi was at the rink with Anna, Kate, Woody, and Max.

"Dad will be sorry he closed the pro shop today," Anna said. "The rink is super-crowded."

"Great!" Randi cried. "The more kids the better! I just hope I haven't forgotten anything."

Randi glanced around the locker room at all the stuff she had brought to the rink. Her six skating posters. The green bag of dresses. The silver trophy. A tall black top hat. And most important of all, her camera.

Randi pulled it out of her pocket and held it up to her eye. "I'm ready. All I have to do is check on Woody and Max."

Randi grabbed the top hat and hurried out of the locker room. She found Woody and Max sitting on a bench in the lobby. "Ready?" she asked them. She handed Woody the top hat.

Woody nodded. "We're ready, but I'm *not* wearing that hat!"

"You have to wear it!" Randi insisted. "People will notice you with the hat on. It will help us get customers." She paused. "We need customers, Woody, or my idea won't work. And if my idea doesn't work . . . *we* will be in big trouble."

Woody groaned. "Aw, all right." He jammed the tall black hat on his head. It was so big, it slid down to his nose and made his ears stick straight out.

Randi and Max clasped their hands over their mouths to keep from giggling. "Remember what I told you to say?" Randi asked.

Woody pulled a crumpled piece of paper from his pocket. "I wrote it down." He pushed the hat up in front so that he could see the words. In a flat voice, he started to read. "Step . . . right . . . up . . . , girls. Today . . . and . . . today . . . only. Dress . . . up—"

"No! Not like that!" Randi cried. "You sound boring!"

"Fine, then I won't do it," Woody grumbled. "This is dumb!"

"No, it isn't!" cried Randi. "Not if you do it right!"

Woody scowled.

"Pretend that you're in the circus," Randi instructed. "Pretend that you're an announcer. Shout it out!" She thought for a second. "I know what will help you! Wait right here."

Randi darted back into the locker room. She yanked one of her posters off the wall. She rolled it into the shape of a giant ice cream cone and went out to the lobby again.

"Yell through this!" she commanded, handing Woody the rolled-up poster. "It will make your voice much louder. And stand on the bench, where everybody can see you!"

"Hey! This is cool!" Woody said, grabbing Randi's homemade megaphone. He hopped up onto the bench. He put the small end of the rolled-up poster to his mouth and yelled—loud and clear. *"Step right up, girls! Today and today only! Dress up like a champion! Get your picture taken! Just five dollars! Inside the locker room!"*

"I'm going back to the locker room," Randi told Max. "Bring everyone who comes to get their picture taken right to the locker room door."

"No problem," Max said.

"Step right up!" Woody's voice filled the lobby.

Three skaters stepped up to Woody. They were fifth-grade girls from Randi's school. Max pointed them in Randi's direction.

Yes! It's working! Randi cheered silently. She ran into the locker room. "Get ready! Here they come!" she told Anna and Kate.

Soon the locker room was jammed full of girls. They all wanted their pictures taken wearing the skating dresses Randi had brought from home. They all wanted to look like champions.

Randi, Anna, and Kate swung into action. They helped the girls change into the skating dresses.

They gave them the trophy to hold.

And Randi took their pictures, standing in front of her posters.

All afternoon girls streamed into the locker room.

All afternoon Randi snapped their pictures.

When the last skater had finally left, Randi grabbed Kate's and Anna's hands. "We'll make enough money to pay for the whole special delivery!" she cried. *And that includes the most important thing of all—Jill's dress!*

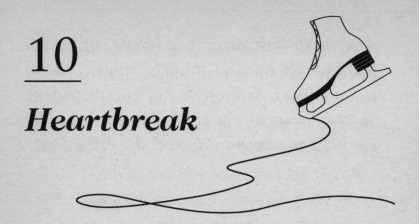

10

Heartbreak

The next morning, Randi woke up and smiled. It was a school holiday. She and all her brothers and sisters had the day off.

Randi sat down at her desk. She took out a piece of paper. On it she wrote,

> To the best skater ever!
> Love,
> Your Number One Fan

Randi pinned the note to the red dress she had chosen for Jill. Then she carefully put the dress back in the bag. She tiptoed down the hallway to Jill's bedroom. Jill's bed was empty. *Perfect!* Randi thought. *Jill will be amazed when she finds this! Just in time for her competition tonight.*

Randi tucked the dress into Jill's closet. Then she pulled on her old jeans and faded sweatshirt and hurried downstairs for breakfast.

Mrs. Wong sat at the kitchen table reading the newspaper. Randi remembered that her mom was also taking the day off.

"Where is everybody, Mom?" she asked.

"Well, your dad's at work," Mrs. Wong answered. "Jill's getting her hair cut. Laurie and the twins are playing at a friend's house. Kristi's at *her* friend's house. And Henry is at soccer practice." She folded the paper. "What are *you* doing today?"

"Meeting Anna at the rink," Randi answered. "But will you take me to the mall first? I want to get my film developed."

"Tell you what," Mrs. Wong said. "I'll drop you off at the camera store, do some shopping, and pick you up when I finish."

When they got to the mall, Randi raced to the camera store. "May I help you?" asked a man with a droopy mustache.

Randi handed him her camera. "I took some really important pictures," she said. "Can you please develop them right away?"

"Sure," the man said, smiling. "They'll be ready in about one hour. Why don't you come back then?"

"I'll wait right here," Randi said. "I want to see my pictures the minute they're developed."

"Okay," the man said. He handed Randi a photo magazine. "Here's something to look at while you wait." He turned and disappeared into a back room.

Randi opened the magazine. But she was much too excited to concentrate on the pictures in it. Today was the day she would pay for the special delivery! Today was the day she would get out of trouble! Today was the day Jill would find her new dress!

Randi glanced up. The man with the mustache came back toward her, holding her camera. "I'm afraid I have bad news. I can't develop your pictures for you."

"Is it because we haven't paid?" Randi said. "My mom will be right back. She'll pay for the pictures then."

"No. That's not it. There's nothing on this film. It looks like someone forgot to take the cover off the lens when they took the pictures."

For a second Randi didn't speak. She couldn't. She felt as if she had just been punched in the stomach. Hard.

How could she be so stupid? How could she forget to take the cover off the lens? How could she ruin her own plan? She burst into tears.

Her mother walked into the store a moment later. "Randi!" Mrs. Wong cried, rushing over to her. "What's wrong?"

Randi looked at her mother through her tears. "I . . . I didn't take the lens cap off my camera. I didn't take any pictures."

"Oh, dear," Mrs. Wong said. She brushed a strand of damp hair out of Randi's eyes. "Well," she said. "You can take more."

"No, I can't, Mom," Randi wailed. "Not like these."

"What were they pictures of?" Mrs. Wong asked.

Randi couldn't tell her mother she had taken the pictures to pay for the special delivery. "They were of . . . of friends," she mumbled.

Mrs. Wong reached into her purse and handed Randi a tissue. "You can take pictures of your friends anytime. Cheer up!"

But Randi couldn't cheer up. She was still upset when her mother dropped her off at the arena. Randi met Anna and Woody just outside the main doors.

"Hey! Did you get the pictures?" Anna asked. "Let me see!"

"You must have taken a zillion of them," Woody said. "That's how many girls Max and I sent to the locker room."

Randi glanced from Anna to Woody. How could she admit her mistake?

"Come on. Let's see them," Anna said.

Randi stared at her feet. "I didn't get *any* pictures," she mumbled. "Not one. I forgot to take the lens cover off the camera when I took them."

"I wore that stupid hat for nothing!" Woody yelled.

Randi felt so embarrassed. "Sorry," she muttered.

"So, if we don't have pictures to sell, that means we don't have money to pay Dad. Right?" Anna said.

Randi nodded. "I tried really hard, but none of my plans worked. I guess it's time to tell your dad the truth."

"Yeah," Anna agreed. She squeezed

Randi's hand. "Hey! Maybe Dad won't be as mad as you think."

"I don't know," Randi said sadly. "I think he might—"

"Special delivery!" someone called.

Randi spun around.

An enormous flatbed truck pulled up in front of the arena. A man hopped out. "Is this the Seneca Hills Ice Arena?" he yelled.

Randi glanced at the truck and gasped. There, on the back of the truck, sat a brand-new, shiny Zamboni.

Randi's eyes popped wide open. "Oh, no!" she cried. "We ordered a Zamboni!"

11

Serious Trouble

Randi felt sick. "A Zamboni!" she wailed. "It's so big! It must cost millions of dollars!"

Woody shook his head. "Whoa! This is serious!"

"What are we going to do, guys?" Randi moaned.

"Now we can't tell Dad," Anna said, sounding very nervous. "He might understand about the dresses. But he'll *never* understand about a Zamboni!"

"No," Randi told Anna. "We have to

tell your dad." She felt really scared. "I'll do it, Anna. I'll tell him. It was mostly my—"

Randi stopped short as the arena door flew open. Mac, the handyman, rushed passed her. "My Zamboni!" he yelled. "I ordered it weeks ago and it finally came!" He ran over to the flatbed truck and gazed lovingly at the new Zamboni.

Randi turned to Anna. Then she turned to Woody. They all burst out laughing. They laughed until their sides ached.

"At least we didn't order *that* special delivery!" Randi finally said. "Let's go tell Mr. Mullen what we *did* order."

Woody nodded. "Yeah. Might as well get it over with."

Randi's stomach churned all the way to the pro shop. *I hope Mr. Mullen understands. I'll promise him I'll never touch his computer again. Ever! Ever! Ever!*

"I've been looking for you, Anna," Mr.

Mullen said when Randi, Anna, and Woody walked into the shop. "I've got some really strange charges on my credit card bill. Did you sign a delivery slip for dresses or warm-up outfits or—"

"Excuse me, Mr. Mullen." Randi's heart thumped in her chest. Her mouth felt as dry as sand. "I can explain the charges."

"You can?" Anna's father asked.

"Yes," Randi said. "It's our fault. Woody's and mine."

"Mostly hers," Woody mumbled.

Randi shot Woody a look. Then she continued, "Woody and I played on your computer that day you ordered the skates. Anna told us not to, but we did it anyway. We thought we were just *looking* at all the equipment. But we must have been *ordering* it. We didn't mean to. Really we didn't."

Mr. Mullen frowned. "I'm disappointed in all of you. I thought you were more responsible than that."

"We tried to send it all back," Randi continued. "But we couldn't find an address. So we hid everything until we could find a way to get rid of it. Then we tried to sell it. But no one answered our message on the computer, so—"

"You tried to sell it on the computer?" Mr. Mullen repeated.

"Yes. But it didn't work. So I had the idea of taking pictures of girls wearing the skating outfits and holding the trophy. If they bought their pictures, then we'd have lots of money to *pay* for everything. It was a great idea . . . except for one little thing."

"One *big* thing," Woody muttered.

Randi hung her head. "I forgot to take the lens cover off my camera. I didn't get one picture. Not one."

"You took all those pictures, and you forgot to take the lens cover off?" Mr. Mullen repeated. "I can't believe it!" He smiled a little. He chuckled. Then he laughed really hard.

"Aren't you mad?" Randi asked. "Aren't

you going to keep us out of your shop for-
ever?"

"Well," Mr. Mullen said, "you shouldn't
have played on my computer without permis-
sion." He paused. "But I know you made a
mistake. You didn't mean to place an order."

"I'm really sorry," Randi burst out.

"So am I," Woody added.

"But you didn't have to do all that crazy
stuff to hide the delivery," Anna's father said.
"All you had to do was tell me. I can send
everything back. No problem." He looked at
Randi. "You do still *have* everything, don't
you?"

"Yes," Randi answered.

"Okay," Mr. Mullen said. "Here's what
we'll do. You three go get all the stuff you've
hidden. Then I want you to pack it neatly in
the boxes so I can send it back."

"It's a deal!" Randi cried.

For the next half hour, Randi, Anna and
Woody raced back and forth among the pro
shop, the locker room, Mrs. Bowen's office,

and Harry's Snack Bar. They collected all the special delivery orders.

"Whew! That's everything," Randi said, out of breath. Then she remembered the bag of dresses in Laurie's closet—and Jill's dress. "Uh, I mean, this is *almost* everything. There's still some stuff at my house."

"We'd better drive over and pick it up," Mr. Mullen said. "I want to send the whole order back this afternoon."

Good thing Jill's out, Randi thought as Mr. Mullen drove her home. *I'll take the dress out of her closet before she even sees it.*

"I'll just be a minute!" Randi said when Anna's father parked in front of her house. She dashed up the walk and through the front door.

"Oh, no!" Randi wailed when she stepped into the living room.

There was Jill, gazing at herself in the mirror. And she was wearing the red dress!

12

Oops!

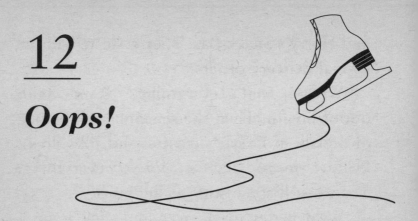

"**R**andi! Don't you just love the dress Mom bought me?" Jill squealed. She turned from side to side.

"Uh . . . yeah. It's . . . it's beautiful," Randi stammered.

But Mom didn't give it to you. I did, she thought.

Jill clasped her hands together. "I can't wait for the competition! I'm going to look so great!"

Randi felt terrible. Jill was so excited. How could Randi tell her she had to give the dress back to Mr. Mullen?

"Jill," Randi began. "I have to tell you—"

"I'm so glad you like your new dress, Jill," Mrs. Wong said as she walked into the living room. "I found it on sale this afternoon at the mall. It looked just like the one in the picture you showed me. It still cost a bit, but it will be worth every penny to see you wear it to the competition."

"Uh, excuse me," Randi said. "Mr. Mullen is waiting outside. I just have to get something." She bounded up the stairs and into Jill's bedroom. She threw open the closet door. There, right where she had tucked it that morning, was the red dress!

Randi grabbed the dress and raced to her room. She stuffed it into the shopping bag and ran downstairs. "Mr. Mullen is driving me back to the rink," she yelled as she ran out the door.

"Good. We'll all meet you there later for Jill's competition," her mother called back.

* * *

"Thanks for still letting me help in your shop, Mr. Mullen," Randi said. She taped up the last of the special delivery boxes.

"Well, you learned your lesson—" Mr. Mullen began.

"Special delivery!" a strange voice interrupted. Randi turned and saw a delivery man standing in the doorway.

Mr. Mullen looked straight at Randi. "Is there something else you ordered that you haven't told me about?"

Randi shook her head. "No. I've told you *everything.*"

"Says here you ordered a Zamboni," the delivery man said.

"A *Zamboni!*" Mr. Mullen shouted.

Randi and Woody looked at each other in horror.

"Uh . . . does the Zamboni have red and white stripes?" Woody asked in a small voice.

"And blue-and-white stars?" Randi added in an even smaller voice.

"Yup," the delivery man said. "And a big red bow on top."

"Uh-oh!" Randi looked at Woody. Woody looked back at Randi. Their faces turned the same color as the big red bow.

"Looks like we'll have to pack this up too," Woody said.

Randi giggled. "But there's no box big enough for *this* special delivery mess!"

About the Author

Effin Older is the author of many children's books published in the United States and abroad.

Effin lived in New Zealand for fourteen years. She currently lives in a tiny village in Vermont with her husband, Jules, and her white husky, Sophie. She has twin daughters named Amber and Willow.

When Effin isn't writing children's books, she likes to take long walks with Sophie, ride her mountain bike, and cross-country ski.

If you glided right through

jump into the SILVER BLADES Series,
featuring Randi Wong's big sister Jill
and her friends.

Look for these titles at your bookstore or library:

BREAKING THE ICE
IN THE SPOTLIGHT
THE COMPETITION
GOING FOR THE GOLD
THE PERFECT PAIR
SKATING CAMP
THE ICE PRINCESS
RUMORS AT THE RINK
SPRING BREAK
CENTER ICE
A SURPRISE TWIST
THE WINNING SPIRIT
THE BIG AUDITION
NUTCRACKER ON ICE
RINKSIDE ROMANCE
A NEW MOVE
ICE MAGIC
A LEAP AHEAD
MORE THAN FRIENDS
WEDDING SECRETS

and coming soon:
NATALIA COMES TO AMERICA